Peppa Pig

Sing with Peppa!

Table of Contents

Adapted by Kathy Broderick

we make books come alive®

pi kids **Phoenix International Publications, Inc.**

Chicago • London • New York • Hamburg • Mexico City • Paris • Sydney

Hooray! Let's sing along with Peppa Pig and all her friends!

Press the colored buttons on your microphone in the order shown to hear the melodies!

Bing Bong Song

We're playing a tune,
   And we're singing a song,
With a bing and a bong and a bir
   Bong bing boo!
Bing bong bing!
   Bing bong bingley bungley b

Then look for special things in the pictures... like a guitar and a recorder!

3

If You're Happy and You Know It

If you're happy and you know it, clap your hands.
If you're happy and you know it, clap your hands.
   If you're happy and you know it,
   And you really want to show it.
If you're happy and you know it, clap your hands.

Big Balloon

Big balloon, big balloon,
   Bigger than the sun and moon,
Flying high, in the sky,
   Fly and fly and fly and fly.

& away
a way
up
up

Now find
a little bird!

5

Rig-a-Jig-Jig

Rig-a-jig-jig and away we go,
    Away we go, away we go.
Rig-a-jig-jig and away we go,
    Hooray, hooray, hooray!

Look for
the pink-and-
white flower.

Now find the green recycling bin.

Recycling Song

Recycle, recycle, we're going to recycle,
Tin cans, bottles, newspapers!
Recycle, recycle, we're going to recycle.

Make New Friends

Make new friends,
    But keep the old.
One is silver,
    And the other is gold.

Look for Peppa's friend Suzy Sheep.

Now find George's dinosaur.

Dinosaur Stomp Song

Do the stomp,
  Do the dinosaur stomp.
Do the roar,
  Do the dinosaur roar.
Stomp, stomp, stomp!
  Roar, roar, roar!
Do the dinosaur stomp. Stomp! Roar!

How many raindrops can you count?

Rain, Rain, Go Away

Rain, rain, go away.
    Come again some other day.
We want to go outside and play.
    Rain, rain, go away.

Muddy Puddles

Jumping up and down
   In muddy puddles,
Splish, splash, splosh, splish, splash!

Jumping up and down
   In muddy puddles,
Splish, splash, splosh, splish, splash!

How many
rain hats
do you see?

MUDDY PUDDLES

Did You Ever See a Princess?

Did you ever see a princess,
　　A princess, a princess?
Did you ever see a princess,
　　Look this way and that?

How many wheels are on Princess Peppa's carriage?

What color are Peppa's shoes?

Lavender's Blue

Lavender's blue, dilly dilly,
Lavender's green.
When I am king, dilly dilly,
You shall be queen.

Girls and Boys, Come Out to Play

Girls and boys, come out to play.
   The moon is shining as bright as day.
Leave your supper and leave your sleep,
   And come in your costumes to Peppa's street.

Look for
a witch's hat.
Now find a
black cat.

Ring a Ring o' Roses

Ring a ring o' roses,
   A pocketful of posies.
A-tishoo! A-tishoo!
   We all fall down.

Look for the black-and-yellow bee.

16

Now find yellow in the rainbow!

JUMP IN!

Rainbow Song

It's a rainy, sunny day.
    The rainbow's here to play.
Rainbow, rainbow,
    Red and orange and yellow and
        green and purple and blue!
Rainbow, rainbow,
    It's a rainy, sunny day!

Can you find Daddy Pig's shoes?

Snort, Snort! What Can the Matter Be?

Snort, snort! What can the matter be?
Snort, snort! What can the matter be?
Snort, snort! What can the matter be?
Daddy Pig's stuck in the door!

The Wheels on the Bus

The wheels on the bus go round and round,
  Round and round, round and round.
The wheels on the bus go round and round,
  All through the town!

Now find three red-and-green watermelons.

Good Morning to You

Good morning to you.

Good morning to you.

Good morning, dear children.

Good morning to you.

Head and Shoulders, Knees and Toes

Head and shoulders, knees and toes, knees and toes.
Head and shoulders, knees and toes, knees and toes.
My eyes and ears and mouth and nose,
Head and shoulders, knees and toes, knees and toes.

Now find the friend wearing polka dots!

The Pirate Ship

I saw a ship a-sailing,
A-sailing on the sea.
And oh, it was all filled up
With friends and fun for me.

AHOY!

Look for the red pirate flag.

ME

MATEY

Now find George's purple glasses!

GEORGE'S ADVENTURE

Row, Row, Row Your Boat

Row, row, row your boat,
    Gently down the stream.
Merrily, merrily, merrily, merrily,
    Life is but a dream.

23

Birdy Birdy, Woof Woof

The birds go woof and the dogs go tweet,
　　Woof tweet, woof tweet, woof woof woof!
The sheep go moo, and the cows go baa,
　　Moo baa woof tweet, woof baa moo tweet,
Woof woof woof!

Find a blue feather.

woo

tweet

moo

baa

Now spot a purple cupcake.

Mummy, Put the Kettle On

Mummy, put the kettle on.
Mummy, put the kettle on.
Mummy, put the kettle on.
    We'll all have tea.

Look for the shooting star.

North Star

North Star, North Star,
   Are you near or are you far?
Can we get there in the car?
   North Star, North Star,
Shining with a twinkly glow,
   Please show us the way to go.